The New Adventures of
MARY-KATE & ASHLEY ™

The Case Of The
HAUNTED MAZE

D0112055

Look for more great books in

series:

The Case Of The
HAUNTED MAZE

by Marilyn Kaye

HarperEntertainment
An Imprint of HarperCollins*Publishers*

A PARACHUTE PRESS BOOK

PARACHUTE PRESS

Parachute Publishing, L.L.C.
156 Fifth Avenue
New York, NY 10010

DUALSTAR PUBLICATIONS

Dualstar Publications
1801 Century Park East
12th Floor
Los Angeles, CA 90067

♨HarperEntertainment

An Imprint of HarperCollins*Publishers*
10 East 53rd Street, New York, NY 10022

www.mary-kateandashley.com

10 9 8 7 6 5 4 3 2 1

HALLOWEEN HOLIDAY

"So, where is the famous maze?" I asked my friend Mitch Mason.

Mitch, my sister Ashley, and I stood on the back porch of Mitch's house. The two of us were visiting Mitch's family farm. The air was crisp, and the leaves had already begun turning colors. It was the perfect place to spend Halloween.

Mitch plopped onto the porch swing. His red hair sparkled in the sunlight. "The maze is behind the barn," he said finally. He grabbed a handful of candy corn from a bowl on the table next to him and popped some into his mouth.

Mitch used to go to our school before his family moved. All year long Mitch wrote us e-mails about his new life on the farm. He wrote a *lot* about the maze. It was made of rows of tall shrubs planted close together in twisting, turning paths and dead ends. People were always stopping by to try to find their way through it.

We wrote Mitch too—about all the mysteries we solve. We had plenty to write about! Ashley and I are the Trenchcoat Twins. We run the Olsen and Olsen Detective Agency. Our office is in the attic of our house.

"You wrote us so much about the maze, we can't wait to see it," Ashley said.

Mitch gave himself a little push on the porch swing. "Don't you want to see the farm animals first?" he asked.

"Farm animals?" Ashley said. Her blue eyes sparkled. She loves all kinds of animals.

Mitch smiled at Ashley. "Sure," he said. He hopped off the swing. "We'll check out the ducks first, and then we'll go to the barn to see the horses."

Mitch led us down a little hill, and we came to a pond. A teenage girl in a pink sweater and blue jeans stood beside the water with a little boy. Her long hair was the same color as Mitch's. Red. She was handing the little boy bits of bread so that he could feed the ducks.

"Remember my sister, Rachel?" Mitch whispered to us. He put a finger to his lips and tiptoed up behind her. As soon as he was almost on top of her he yelled, "Quack! Quack!"

It wasn't a very good duck imitation, but it startled his sister. She let out a shriek and whirled around. The little boy started giggling, but Rachel scowled.

"That wasn't funny, Mitch!" Rachel scolded.

"Yes, it was," Mitch said, laughing.

Ashley and I gave each other knowing looks. Mitch hadn't changed in the past year. He always played pranks at school. Obviously he still loved being a joker.

I looked down at the little boy. "What's your name?" I asked him.

"Nicky," he said. "Rachel is my babysitter." He tugged at Rachel's hand. "Come on, Rachel. We have to look for Chuckles."

"Who is Chuckles?" Ashley asked.

"It's his favorite toy," Rachel replied. "He lost it."

"Chuckles has been gone for so long!" Nicky said. He looked as if he was about to cry.

"The toy vanished about a week ago," Rachel explained to us. She patted Nicky's head. "Don't worry, Nicky. Chuckles will turn up. Want to go say hello to the horses?"

"That's where we're headed too," Mitch said.

"Maybe we should see the maze now," Ashley suggested. She looked up at the sky. "The sun will set soon."

"Later, okay?" Mitch turned and headed back up the path toward the barn.

Ashley's forehead crinkled with confusion, then she shrugged. "Okay."

That's strange, I thought. *It seems as if Mitch doesn't want to show us the maze.*

As we entered the barn, my nose wrinkled from all the different smells: hay, freshly cut grass, and the two beautiful horses.

Nicky immediately started making a big hay pile.

Ashley bent down to stroke a small white pig that was sniffing at her feet. "He's so cute!" she declared.

"We call him Wilbur," Rachel told her. "Like the pig in *Charlotte's Web*."

"And that's Charlotte, the spider, spinning a web right above Rachel's head," Mitch said, pointing up at the rafters.

Rachel gasped and covered her head with her arms. "A spider? Is it going to land in my hair?" One look at Mitch's expression told her that this was just another prank. Her eyes narrowed. She was even madder than she'd been at the duck pond.

"Rachel's scared of spiders," Mitch told us with a grin.

Rachel glared at him. "I'm not the only one around here who's afraid of something. Are you going to show your friends the maze, Mitch? Or are you too scared?"

Mitch didn't answer her. He shoved his hands into his jacket pockets and stared down at his sneakers.

Rachel took Nicky's hand. "Come on, Nicky. It's time for us to meet your brother."

"And it's time we find out why Mitch is afraid of the maze," I whispered to Ashley.

Ashley nodded. We all followed Rachel and Nicky out of the barn.

"I think you have a fan," Rachel told Ashley. She nodded at Wilbur, who was trotting alongside Ashley.

"He acts like a puppy," Ashley said. "Does he do tricks?"

Before Rachel could answer, a figure on a skateboard seemed to zoom out of nowhere.

Wilbur squealed and ran back into the barn.

Twisting and turning and doing a couple of fancy moves, the skateboarder suddenly was on a direct course to crash into Rachel!

"Hey! Watch out!" I cried.

Rachel gasped.

Then, at the last second, the skateboarder made a sharp turn away from her and hopped off his board.

Rachel stamped one foot. "You almost ran me down!"

Mitch laughed. "Good one, Jared!"

"I should have come after *you*," Jared told Mitch. "As payback for all your practical jokes on *me*."

"You boys and your stupid pranks!" Rachel fumed. "See you tomorrow, Nicky." She left the little boy with his older brother and stomped off toward the house.

Jared tucked his skateboard under one arm and took his little brother by the hand. "Let's go home," he said, turning toward the white farmhouse across the road, where they lived.

"We still didn't find Chuckles," Nicky complained.

"He'll turn up soon," Jared said.

"Can we see if he's in the maze?" Nicky asked.

I glanced at Mitch. He jiggled his pockets nervously. A mere mention of the maze seemed to make him nervous.

"Sure," Jared said. "We'll ask Rachel to look for Chuckles in the maze tomorrow."

"Jared doesn't like going into the maze," Nicky told us.

So Mitch isn't the only one with maze problems, I thought. Curious, I asked, "Why don't you like the maze, Jared?"

Jared shrugged. "It's not that I don't like it," he explained. "I just get so mixed up in there."

"He always gets lost," Nicky said. "No matter how many times he tries."

Jared looked a little embarrassed. "Ready, kiddo?" he asked Nicky. "Later," Jared said to us. Then he and Nicky turned around and headed home.

"*Now* can we check out the maze?" I asked.

"Anybody thirsty?" Mitch asked. "Want to go back to the house and grab some sodas?"

Ashley faced him squarely. "Mitch, you keep changing the subject. Why don't you want to take us to see the maze?"

"And why did your sister say you're afraid of it?" I asked.

Mitch's face turned red—almost as red as his hair. "I . . . uh . . . well . . ." His voice trailed off.

"Well *what*?" Ashley demanded.

"I guess I'd better tell you," he said. He looked straight at us, his brown eyes big and serious. "About the maze . . ."

He took a deep breath.

"It's haunted."

2

INTO THE MAZE

"**H**aunted!" I said. "You mean, there's a ghost in the maze?"

"You never wrote us about that!" Ashley said.

"I only just found out about it last week," Mitch said. "I was walking through the maze when I heard rustling sounds behind me, as if someone or something was following me. Then I heard very strange laughing."

"Someone must have come into the maze after you," Ashley said.

Mitch shook his head. "There wasn't anyone else around when I went in. And that laugh!" He shivered. "It didn't sound like any *human* laugh I'd ever heard."

I could feel little goose bumps running along my arms. I looked toward the tall hedges that made the maze walls. *Maybe we shouldn't go into the maze, after all!* I thought.

"It couldn't have been a ghost, Mitch," Ashley declared. "There's no such thing."

"That's what I thought too," Mitch said. "But then I saw it! It was floating in the air, right above the hedges!"

Ashley shook her head. "Just because you saw something weird in the maze once doesn't mean it's haunted, Mitch."

"I didn't see it just once," Mitch argued. "I saw it *twice*."

Ashley rolled her eyes and raised an eyebrow at me.

I knew exactly what she was thinking.

This was another one of Mitch's pranks. Of course! He thought he could fool us into believing the maze was haunted. And I almost fell for it!

"Well, I'm not afraid of ghosts," I announced. I wasn't going to let him fool me one minute longer. "Let's go to the maze right now and meet your 'ghost.'"

Mitch sighed. "Okay. But let's be quick. It's going to get dark pretty soon."

We hurried alongside Mitch toward the maze. The hedges that made up the maze walls were so tall that I couldn't see over the tops of them. The tiny green leaves of the shrubs grew so closely together, the only way in or out of the maze was through the entrance. *Still*, I thought, *how hard could it be to find your way through a bunch of bushes?*

A young man with black hair and glasses stood outside the entrance to the maze. He held a small wooden step stool. A large trash bag sat on the ground beside him. There were a few twigs stuck to his overalls.

"That's the caretaker," Mitch whispered to us. "We call him Greavy, but 'Grumpy' is more like it!" He called out to the man. "Greavy! I'm going to show my friends the maze!"

Greavy frowned. "I just cleaned it. You kids better not make a mess in there."

"We won't," Ashley promised.

"Of course, we can't speak for the ghost," I joked.

The caretaker's frown deepened. "What do *you* know about the ghost?"

I was startled. "You mean . . . there really *is* a ghost?" I never expected someone else to go along with one of Mitch's jokes!

"Tell them about the legend, Greavy," Mitch urged.

The grumpy caretaker opened the step stool and sat down on the top step. "Are you sure you want to hear it?" he asked.

"We're sure," Ashley said, and I nodded.

"It was a hundred years ago, on a Halloween night," he began. "There was only this one farm around here, and there was the maze. No one knew who made it or how long ago." He paused.

I glanced at Mitch. He was nodding. *I guess he's heard this story before*, I thought.

"A young couple was living here, with a son and a slightly older daughter about your age," Greavy said. He looked at Mitch. "In fact, the boy had curly red hair just like you."

Mitch bit his lower lip.

"Their parents forbade the boy and girl to go into the maze alone," Greavy continued.

"Why?" I asked.

"You can get lost in there," he said. "You could just walk around and around without getting anywhere. Ever."

A shiver ran down my back.

"Anyway, one night after supper the boy went into the maze alone—on a dare," Greavy went on. "When he didn't come back well after dark, his sister went into the maze looking for him. Their parents became frantic when they realized their children were missing. Later that night the boy came home, tired and cold from wandering all the twists and turns of the maze for so long. But the boy never saw his sister in there. Neither did the parents when they searched the maze."

My eyes widened. "She never came home? Ever?"

"Nope." The caretaker shrugged. "Guess she got lost in the maze. Forever."

Ashley gazed at Greavy in horror. "Didn't people search for her?"

"Sure," he said. "But no one ever saw her again. Well, not exactly . . ."

Okay, now he was officially giving me the creeps. "What do you mean?" I asked.

"People say that her ghost haunts the maze to this day. She shows up every ten years. Everyone says she's still looking for her little brother. I guess she doesn't know that he made it safely out of the maze—one hundred years ago."

Mitch gulped.

"Has anyone actually seen this ghost?" I asked.

"Someone must have," Greavy said. "For years there's been talk of what the ghost looks like. She's dressed all in white, they say, with long blond hair."

"And she's looking for a red-haired boy our age," Ashley said thoughtfully.

Mitch's hands went up to touch the red curls on his head.

"Folks around here take their legends seriously," Greavy said. "The last time the ghost showed up, not a single red-haired boy would go into the maze. And that was back when the maze just became a huge attraction."

"When was that exactly?" Ashley asked.

"Well, let's see, it was around the time the new high school opened," Greavy said. "That would have been . . . ten years ago."

We were all silent.

"You kids still want to go in there?" Greavy asked.

"Yes," Ashley declared. I nodded, and after a moment Mitch did too.

"Suit yourself," Greavy said. He stood and picked up the wooden step stool. "Just don't leave anything behind in there, and don't mess with the shrubs."

"We won't," Mitch promised.

Greavy gave us a long, hard look. Then he grabbed the trash bag and slowly walked away.

We watched him for a moment, then turned and stared at the entrance to the maze. No one said anything. I think we were all shook up by Greavy's story, but none of us wanted to admit it.

"You know," I said finally, "someone could have just made up that story, and people kept repeating it as if it were true. That's how legends get started."

"That's right," Ashley said. "Come on. Let's do some ghost hunting!" She laughed to show she didn't believe in the ghost.

We faced the entrance. The dirt path was narrow, so we were going to have to walk in single file.

"I'll go first," Ashley announced. To me she whispered, "That way Mitch can't plant anything in our path to scare us."

I nodded. I could see that she still thought the whole ghost idea was one of Mitch's pranks. I wasn't so sure, so I was glad that Ashley volunteered to go first. I followed Ashley, and Mitch followed me.

Even though the sun hadn't set yet, the tall hedges blocked out the light. We could barely see where we were going. The only sounds were our muffled footsteps and insect chirps—probably grasshoppers or crickets.

Surrounded by the tall hedges, we walked a few feet. Then the path before us branched into a *T*.

"Which way should we go?" I whispered. Something about the maze made me keep my voice very low.

"To the right," Mitch said.

"Are you sure?" I asked. I wondered if Mitch had set up a trick in that direction.

Ashley must have had the same idea. "We'll go left," she decided.

"Honest, you guys. Right is the easiest way to go," Mitch said. His voice was shaky. He seemed to be truly nervous.

I looked at Ashley. She shook her head, so we turned left. A squirrel scurried past us, and we all jumped.

I giggled. "Well, it looks as if the squirrel knows his way around!" I joked. "If we get lost, we can just follow him!"

"Ha-ha," Mitch said. "Very funny."

We kept walking. The tall, leafy walls loomed over us.

The farther we went into the maze, the darker it seemed to get. The uneven tops of the hedge walls cast creepy shadows on the dirt pathways.

Suddenly we faced a wall of leaves again. We had to turn one way or the other.

"We'll go right," Ashley said. She didn't sound so sure of herself this time. "Is that okay with you, Mary-Kate?"

"Yeah, sure," I said. My own voice sounded a little shaky. "What do you think, Mitch?"

There was no reply.

"Mitch?"

No answer. Ashley and I turned around.

Mitch was gone!

SAME OLD MITCH?

"**M**itch! Mitch!" I cried. "Where are you?"

"He just disappeared," Ashley said. She shook her head. "But that's impossible! He must have turned and we didn't notice."

"Or maybe he climbed up the hedge wall," I suggested. I gazed up and gasped. "Ashley—look!"

Above our heads, near the top of the hedge, two glowing eyes peered down at us.

"He . . . hello? Who . . . who are you?" I asked. I tried to sound braver than I felt, but my voice was shaking. "He . . . hello?"

Silence.

As we stared at the eyes, they blinked. Then they disappeared.

"Ghost eyes," I whispered. "Ashley, those were ghost eyes!" A rustling sound nearby made us both freeze. "What was that?" I whispered.

"I-I don't know," Ashley stammered.

"We have to get out of here," I said.

Ashley didn't want to leave yet. "Wait," she said. "Don't you see what's going on? It's a prank! Mitch is trying to scare us!"

"Well, it's working," I said.

"Let's find him and catch him in the act," Ashley said. She closed her eyes and concentrated hard. "Listen. Can you tell which direction that rustling is coming from?" she asked.

I shut my eyes too and listened. "That way." I opened my eyes and pointed through an archway in the maze.

"Let's go!" Ashley said, pulling on my

sweat shirt sleeve. "I'll bet it's Mitch!"

We tried to follow the sounds, but we couldn't find a path that led in the right direction. I noticed something in the dirt.

"Footprints!" I said.

There were clear marks shaped like sneakers on a side path. Ghosts didn't wear sneakers, but Mitch did.

Ashley suddenly stopped. "What's that?" she asked. She looked closely at a branch in the maze wall. Something pink and fluffy was stuck to it.

"Didn't Greavy say he just cleaned the maze?" I said.

"So this hasn't been here very long," Ashley decided. She took the pink fluff and put it into her jacket pocket. Then we went on following the sneaker prints.

Now I was the one who stopped. "Wait a minute," I said. "Look, Ashley! Here are more footprints."

Ashley knelt down and examined them.

Then she stood, raised her right foot, and stuck it into one of the footprints. It fit perfectly.

"These are *our* footprints, Mary-Kate," she said. "We're walking in circles!"

I thought about the blond-haired girl in the legend. We were lost, just like she was. What if we couldn't find our way out either? Ten years from now, would people still be talking about the sisters who disappeared in the maze?

"Ashley! Mary-Kate!"

We whirled around.

It was Mitch, and his face was white. "Guys, I saw it! I saw the ghost!"

Ashley and I looked at each other. Who was he kidding?

I put my hands on my hips. "Yeah, sure," I said. "What did the ghost look like?"

Mitch stared past me, above my head. He raised a shaking arm and pointed.

"Like—like *that*!" he said.

4

MORE CLUES

I couldn't believe my eyes. There, floating in the dark sky just above the top of the hedge was a figure, cloaked in white with long, straight blond hair.

Then we heard a weird, cackling laugh. My stomach flip-flopped.

"Let's get out of here!" Mitch yelled.

We didn't argue with that!

We raced after Mitch as fast as we could, to the right, to the left, to the right again. I was completely confused. I sure hoped

Mitch knew the way out! I couldn't tell whether the ghost was following us. I was afraid to slow down to look over my shoulder.

We burst out of the maze. We stopped for a moment to catch our breath, and I worked up the nerve to look back. There was no sign of the ghost.

"*Now* do you believe me?" Mitch asked. "There really is a ghost!"

No kidding, I thought. *I just saw it for myself!*

Ashley wasn't so sure. "Okay, Mitch, so *you're* not the ghost. But that doesn't mean the ghost is *real*."

"It looked like a real ghost to me," I said. "It even had long blond hair, just like the girl in the legend."

I glanced back at the maze and shivered. The sun had set, and the hedges were nearly black in the inky twilight.

"There's no such thing as ghosts," Ashley

said sternly. "Someone was probably just trying to scare us."

"Can we go back to the house now, please?" Mitch said.

I could see he was pretty shaken up. Who could blame him?

We turned our backs on the maze and headed up the path toward the house.

"Why would anyone want to scare us?" I asked.

Ashley shrugged. "I guess the Trenchcoat Twins just found another mystery to solve."

"I don't think it's a mystery," Mitch insisted. "I think it's a ghost."

"It can't be. But whatever it is, we'll figure it out," Ashley promised. "Once and for all."

Suddenly, a figure stepped onto the path in front of us. We all jumped. "You kids didn't leave any trash in the maze, did you?"

It was Greavy. I breathed a sigh of relief.

"No, Greavy," Mitch answered.

"Good. I've got enough work around

here as it is without having to keep an eye on the maze," he said.

"Have a lot of people been visiting the maze lately?" Ashley asked the caretaker.

Greavy sighed. "Too many," he said. "You'd think folks would hear the place was haunted, and they'd stay away."

"I know I would," Mitch said under his breath.

When we got to the house, Ashley and I went upstairs to the guest room we were sharing. Ashley pulled out her detective notebook. She turned to a clean page and wrote *The Case of the Haunted Maze* at the top. She always keeps careful notes whenever we have a case. She's very organized.

"I don't think we have much to write down yet," I told her.

She bit her lower lip and thought. "I still think Mitch is a suspect," she said. She wrote down *Suspects* and then Mitch's name underneath it. "And that this is just one of his annoying pranks," she added.

I shook my head. "I don't think Mitch is pulling a prank," I said. "You saw how scared he was."

"He could just be pretending," Ashley pointed out. "You know how much he loves to play practical jokes."

"But what would his motive be?" I asked. "You know, like *why* would he play a joke like this?"

Ashley shrugged. "For fun?"

I made a face.

"Okay," Ashley said, "scratch Mitch. For *now*," she added, writing *maybe* next to his name.

"You know," I said, "Greavy doesn't seem to like the maze very much. It sounded as if he wished the ghost *would* scare everyone away."

"Great, Mary-Kate!" Ashley grinned at me, then she wrote *Greavy* as suspect number two, and *too much work* as his motive.

I frowned. "We don't really have any clues," I said.

"Hmm." Ashley's forehead wrinkled. Then she hopped up off the bed. She pulled the little piece of pink fluff she'd found in the hedge out of her pocket. "We have this!"

I stared at the fluff. "As clues go, that isn't the best we've ever had."

Ashley laughed. "True," she said. "But at least it's a start." She found a small plastic bag in her suitcase and dropped the fluff into it. "Now let's solve 'The Mystery of the Growling Stomachs' by having dinner!"

The next morning I was groggy. I didn't sleep very well. I kept dreaming about getting lost in the maze and being chased by fluffy pink ghosts!

But Ashley was all set to get started. She had her notebook, a pencil, and several little plastic bags for collecting evidence.

"You really want to go back into the haunted maze?" I asked her. I shuddered as I remembered the horrible ghost laugh.

"I don't think it's haunted," she said firmly. "But there is something going on in that maze, and I want to find out what it is. And," she added, "I think we should look without Mitch around. He is a suspect, after all."

I knew she was right. I tried to ignore the jittery feeling in my stomach.

The maze didn't look so scary in the morning. The bright autumn sunlight made it much easier to believe that the ghost was fake. Still, I was worried. "Ashley, we could get lost in there."

"I thought of that," Ashley said. She pulled a handful of candy corn from her pocket. "I grabbed these from the bowl on the porch. We can drop them along our way and then follow them back out."

"Good thinking," I said. I just hoped that

candy corn wasn't the ghost's favorite food!

We started on our way. Every few steps Ashley dropped a piece of candy corn.

"What exactly are we looking for?" I asked, gazing around at the hedges.

"Clues," Ashley said.

I stuck out my tongue at her. "Duh!" I said.

The creepy, shivery feeling came back as we went deeper into the maze. Ashley studied the ground carefully. I kept looking around, expecting the ghost to pop out from behind a hedge.

The breeze rustled the shrubs' tiny leaves. A glimmer of some long, yellowish strands in the hedge caught my eye. "Ashley, look!" I hurried over to the spot. "It looks like the ghost's hair," I said. Carefully I untangled the strands from the branches.

"Let me see," Ashley said. She took the strands from me and inspected them. "This doesn't feel like real hair to me."

It didn't to me either. "Maybe ghost hair doesn't feel like human hair," I suggested.

Ashley took the strands and placed them in a small plastic bag she pulled from her backpack. Then we moved on.

Ashley was still watching the ground. "Those are the footprints we made yesterday," she said. "But those aren't." She pointed at the dirt path.

I bent down to look. The marks were evenly spaced, like footprints. But they didn't look like feet. They were small and square.

Ashley squatted down next to me. "Can you think of any animal that makes marks like that?"

I shook my head. "Weird. Could they be ghost footprints?"

"I doubt it," Ashley said. "We need to look for something small and square that would make these marks."

"And remember the glowing eyes?" I asked. "What do you think those were?"

"Lights?" Ashley guessed. "Like the kind that are used on Christmas trees?"

"Maybe," I said. "We need to keep looking."

Ashley nodded. But after half an hour we still hadn't found anything to explain away the ghost. Following the candy corn Ashley had dropped, we made our way out of the maze.

"Good thing you brought that candy," I told Ashley. "I don't think we'd ever have gotten out otherwise."

Ashley nodded. "It's really confusing in there."

"I know you don't believe in ghosts, Ashley," I said. "But I don't think we can rule it out. We didn't find anything that proved the ghost was a fake."

Ashley sighed, then pulled out her detective notebook. On the Suspects page, under Mitch and Greavy, she added another one.

Ghost.

5

MORE SUSPECTS

Ashley and I came around the side of the maze and nearly knocked over Greavy.

"Watch it!" he shouted. He was standing on his step stool, trimming the top of the hedge. Luckily he caught his balance and didn't fall.

"Sorry!" I said, backing away from him.

"You kids! Always underfoot," he grumbled. He glared at us. "I suppose you two were in the maze?"

"Yes," I replied. Ashley and I exchanged

looks. "We were careful not to make a mess," I added.

"Well, at least I didn't have to go rescuing you," he said. He shook his head. "That's usually what happens."

"Sounds as if that maze causes you a lot of trouble," Ashley said.

Greavy climbed down from his step stool. "Sure does. First of all, the hedges need to be kept trimmed and tidy." He tossed some branches onto a small pile beside the step stool. "But the worst is all the kids. Getting lost. Leaving trash. Snapping off branches."

"And now there's this ghost," I added. "Does the ghost cause you any other problems?"

Greavy picked up the step stool and moved it a few feet farther down the hedge. "I really thought that with the legend going around again, people would stay away," he said. "But, no. Now they all want to see the famous *haunted* maze."

"There it is!" someone shouted from behind us. "Cool!"

My head whipped around. Three teenagers were walking toward us.

"Can we check out the maze?" a boy wearing a backward baseball cap asked.

Greavy squinted at the threesome. "I suppose I can't say no," he grumbled.

"Excellent!" the girl in the group exclaimed.

"Come with me," Greavy said.

"I think he wishes there really *was* a ghost," Ashley said when they were gone.

"No kidding," I agreed. "He'd be a lot happier if no one came to see the maze."

"It must be a lot of work to keep the hedges so perfectly trimmed," Ashley said. She glanced at the little pile of twigs and leaves that Greavy had dropped. Then her eyes widened.

"Mary-Kate, take a look at this," she said, pointing to the ground. "Look familiar?"

I gazed down at the dirt. "Little square marks!" I smiled at Ashley. "Greavy's step stool makes square marks in the ground like the ones we found in the maze!"

Ashley pulled out her notebook. "He has a motive. And now we have a clue that links him to the ghost."

I studied the prints more closely. "These marks look sort of different," I noted. "They're not spaced the same way as the ones in the maze."

Ashley bit her pencil. "We'll have to double-check."

"Later," I suggested. "When Grumpy Greavy isn't in there."

When we got back to the house, Mitch and his family were just sitting down to breakfast.

"Good morning, Mary-Kate. Good morning, Ashley," Mrs. Mason greeted us. "Sit right down. You're just in time to eat."

Mr. Mason took a big shiny red apple

from the fruit bowl and bit into it. He made a funny face. "Okay, who put a plastic apple into the fruit bowl?" he demanded.

"Who do you think?" Rachel said.

All eyes turned to Mitch. Mitch grinned, and his father shook his head wearily. "Young man, one of these days you'll go too far," he scolded.

"He was probably hoping *I'd* be the one to bite that," Rachel said.

"You really do need to lay off your jokes, Mitch," Mrs. Mason said. "Not everyone finds them as funny as you do." She placed a pitcher of orange juice on the table. "Even your friends are losing their patience."

Mr. Mason helped himself to a biscuit and buttered it. "Is Jared still mad at you for hiding his shoes during gym class last week?"

Mitch shrugged. "Nah," he said. Then he grinned. "Besides, when it comes to pranks, he's almost as good as me!"

"Or as *bad* as you," Rachel said.

After breakfast we helped clear the table.

"We need apples," Mrs. Mason said. "*Real* apples. Does anyone want to go to the farmers' market?"

"I'll go," Rachel volunteered. She grabbed her pink jacket from a peg on the wall near the front door. The jacket matched her headband and her high-top sneakers.

Pink jacket and accessories, I noted. I handed Ashley a clean plate to dry and whispered, "Have you noticed that pink seems to be Rachel's favorite color?"

Her eyes widened. "We'll have to find out what other pink stuff she has," she whispered back.

Once the dishes were washed, Ashley and I grabbed Mitch. We dragged him upstairs and into Rachel's room.

"What's going on?" he asked. "Rachel hates it when I go into her room. If she catches me in here, she'll be super-mad."

"We have to risk it," I said. We told him

about the clues we'd found in the maze.

Ashley took out the plastic bag with the pink fluff. "Rachel likes to wear pink, right? Could this have come from one of her sweaters?"

"You think that Rachel is the ghost?" Mitch asked.

"I don't know," Ashley admitted. "That's why we have to search for more clues."

"Well, she'll be at the farmers' market for at least an hour," Mitch said. "I guess we can look for something that matches the fluff. But let's do it quickly!"

Ashley looked through Rachel's closet. Mitch looked through her drawers. I searched under the bed. We found pink pajamas, pink slippers, and a pink bathrobe. Suddenly, the door to Rachel's room flung open.

Rachel stood in the doorway. Her eyes flashed with fury. "Just what do you think you're doing?" she demanded.

6

To Market, To Market

Mitch gulped. "Uh, I thought you went to the farmers' market," he said.

"I forgot something." Rachel glared at Mitch. "Are you setting up one of your stupid pranks in here, Mitch?"

"No, we—" Mitch started to protest, but Rachel cut him off.

"Get out!" she shouted.

We all hurried out of her room.

We shouldn't let Mitch take the blame for this, I thought. I turned to tell Rachel that it was my idea to go into her room. But then I saw her take something out of her desk. Something orange. I couldn't tell what it was, though. Maybe it really *was* an orange. But why would she keep an orange in her desk?

"Sorry, Rachel," I said. "We just wanted to get a better view of the maze. Mitch said you can see the whole maze from your room."

Rachel frowned. She stuffed the orange thing into her pocket. "Well, I guess it's okay if you and Ashley come into my room. But not Mitch!"

Mitch rolled his eyes. "We were just leaving anyway," he said.

We followed Mitch downstairs and outside. "I don't believe that Rachel is the ghost," Mitch said. "She couldn't pull off something like that. And the pink fluff you found in the maze could be from anybody. Lots of girls wear pink clothes."

A loud shout from behind the barn caught our attention.

"Do you think it's the ghost again?" Mitch asked nervously.

I shook my head. "That sounded more like Greavy."

We hurried around to the back of the barn. Greavy was yelling at the three teenagers who had gone into the maze before breakfast.

"What's going on?" Mitch asked the furious caretaker.

"That one!" Greavy pointed to the girl. "She decided to 'decorate' the maze for Halloween! She made a huge mess in there!"

The girl grinned. "I think a haunted maze is perfect for Halloween, don't you?"

"I don't think *he* thinks it's perfect, Cindy," the boy with the baseball cap said. He nodded toward Greavy.

The other boy rolled his eyes. "Sorry. But our sister has Halloween on the brain."

"This is private property!" Greavy said.

"But the whole town goes into this maze," Cindy pointed out. "That's not very private."

Greavy scowled. "Well, they wouldn't if I had anything to say about it!"

Cindy looked at me and Ashley. "I bet the ghost will think the maze is even better now that it's decorated!"

My eyebrows rose. "What do *you* know about the ghost?"

Cindy laughed. "Everyone knows the legend. And I just made it better!"

"What do you mean?" Ashley asked.

"I'll tell you what she means," Greavy snarled. "She strung up fake cobwebs, cardboard black cats and jack-o'-lanterns, and she stuffed ghosts into the hedges."

"Ghosts?" Mitch repeated. He glanced at Ashley and me.

"When, exactly, did you start putting up decorations?" Ashley asked Cindy.

"Practically before she could walk or talk," one of the boys said.

I laughed. "I think Ashley meant, when did Cindy start decorating the *maze*."

"I wanted to get here yesterday," Cindy explained. "But my stupid brothers made me drive them around on errands all day. I'm the only one with a driver's license."

I guess she couldn't be our ghost if she was driving her brothers around all day, I thought. *She has an alibi.*

"May I see the ghosts you made?" Ashley asked.

"Sure!" Cindy pulled a toy ghost from her backpack. "I used a Styrofoam ball for the head, covered it with a handkerchief, and tied a ribbon around its neck. Isn't it cute?"

It *was* cute. But it definitely did not match the ghost we saw. Maybe Cindy wasn't such a good suspect, after all.

"You go back in there and take down

every single thing you put up!" Greavy insisted.

Cindy sighed. "Okay. I'm sorry. We didn't mean to cause trouble. Come on, guys," she said to her brothers.

We watched them trudge back into the maze.

"We should close this maze down," Greavy said. "Or destroy it! What if those three had gotten lost inside? Or fallen and hurt themselves while sticking up their silly decorations?" He sighed. "I'd better go keep an eye on them."

Greavy vanished into the maze after the trio of teenagers.

"Did you hear that?" I said. "He wishes the maze would be shut down. I bet he thinks a ghost story could do that."

"Well, he thought wrong," Ashley said. "Those kids are here *because* of the story."

Mitch shook his head. "I don't think Greavy is the ghost either," he said.

"Why not?" I asked. "He has a motive, and he has the opportunity—the chance to do whatever he wants in the maze. His step stool makes square marks like the ones we saw on the pathway in there."

"But he wears overalls, not a white gown," Mitch replied. "And he certainly doesn't have long blond hair. Plus, I don't know any *person* who could have made that horrible laugh."

Ashley shook her head. "There's a reasonable explanation for all of this," she insisted. "And we're going to figure out what it is."

"So what should we do now?" I asked.

"We should steer clear of the maze while Greavy is so annoyed," Mitch said. "Why don't we go to the farmers' market too?"

It was a beautiful day, perfect for visiting an open-air market. We walked by the barn and headed for the main road.

Ashley suddenly shrieked and stumbled

forward. "Who did that? Who pushed me?"

I whirled around. Then I burst out laughing. "Wilbur!" I scolded the little pig. "Did you trip Ashley?"

The pig gazed up at me with innocent pink eyes. Then it nuzzled Ashley's knees.

Mitch grinned. "I think Wilbur has a crush on you, Ashley."

Ashley bent down and scratched the pig behind the ears. "I like you too, Wilbur. Just don't sniff my knees so hard." She looked at Mitch. "Can we bring him with us?"

"Okay," Mitch said. "We'll just have to keep on eye on him to make sure he doesn't run off."

I glanced at the pig happily trotting alongside Ashley. "I don't think he'll stray too far from his new best friend."

We headed toward the farmers' market. As we passed Jared and Nicky's house, from across the road we saw a familiar figure in pink heading toward the front door.

"Why is Rachel going to Jared's house?" Mitch wondered.

"Maybe she's babysitting Nicky," I suggested.

Mitch shook his head. "Not until this afternoon."

On a hunch I said, "Let's see what she's up to. Stay out of sight."

We scurried closer and ducked down behind the bushes bordering the yard. Luckily their leaves didn't grow as tightly together as the shrubs of the maze did and we could see through the branches.

Ashley peered through the shrubs. "Rachel's talking to Jared," she reported. "Now she's giving him something. Something orange."

"That must be what I saw her take out of her desk drawer," I said. "What is it?"

"I can't tell," Ashley said. "Now they're both laughing."

"Rachel? Laughing? With Jared?" Mitch

shook his head. "No way. Rachel can't stand Jared. He plays more pranks on her than I do!"

We waited till Rachel left Jared and Nicky's house. After catching us in her room before, we didn't want her to find us spying on her too! As soon as she turned the corner, we came out from our hiding spot behind the bushes and headed for the farmers' market too.

The outdoor market was a cool place. There were lots of stands and tables set up where people who farmed sold all kinds of homegrown or homemade goods.

"Hey, there's Rachel," I said, spotting her pink jacket.

"Looks like she just bought a huge bag of corn on the cob," Mitch said. "Funny, I thought she was here to buy apples."

"She's headed to an apple stand now," I said.

We went to a corn stall, where Mitch

introduced us to one of his classmates, Kelly.

Kelly was really pretty, with long blond hair, freckles, and bright green eyes. She wore blue jeans, a pink and brown sweater, and a pink baseball cap.

"My parents let me sell my crafts here," Kelly told us. She showed us her creations. I loved the animals carved from corncobs. Ashley liked the little dolls Kelly made from the husks, with corn-silk hair.

"Kelly's family owns the cornfield across the road," Mitch told us.

I turned to look at the field. "Wow, that corn is almost as high as the hedges in your maze, Mitch."

Kelly nodded. "I want to turn part of the cornfield into a maze. My parents said if I keep it small and do most of the work myself, it's okay with them."

Mitch frowned. "This town doesn't need two mazes," he said.

"People are going to be too afraid to visit

your maze," Kelly said. "Because of the ghost." She turned to Ashley and me. "I'm going to take a break now. Want to come see my cornfield?"

We crossed the road with Kelly. It was hard to imagine how the forest of corn she showed us could be turned into a maze.

"We'll have to cut down some stalks to make the dead ends and the twisting paths," Kelly said. "Then there will be only one way in and one way out."

Wilbur had no trouble finding a way in. He made a loud snuffling sound, then ran into the cornfield. The tall cornstalks swallowed him up completely.

"I guess he's hungry," Kelly said. "There are still some ears of corn left on the stalks."

"Oh, great," Mitch said. "He'll get lost in there, and it will take us ages to find him."

We all began yelling, "Wilbur! C'mon out, Wilbur!" But Wilbur didn't come back. Not even when Ashley called him.

"I'll get him," I offered. "You stay out here and keep calling."

I squeezed between some cornstalks and pushed aside the heavy leaves. Luckily Wilbur started squealing, so I was able to follow the sound.

"I wonder what has him so excited," I muttered, slipping sideways between stalks. I turned to look around and got hit in the face with cornstalks. "I don't think this cornfield maze idea is so great." I brushed the leaves from my face and continued looking for Wilbur.

Before long I caught up with him. He was digging around the bottom of a cornstalk. Kelly was right. The little pig had a few chewed-up corncobs beside him.

Now how do I get Wilbur out of here? I wondered. *He's way too heavy for me to carry.* I yanked an ear of corn from a stalk and waved it at Wilbur. That got his attention. He trotted toward me.

"Good," I told the piglet. "Now you follow me out."

But there was a problem. I didn't know *how* to get out! There were cornstalks in every direction. When I pushed them aside, I only saw more stalks. The more I looked around, the dizzier I felt. I couldn't even figure out from which direction I'd come!

I hoped my voice would carry through the corn. "Help! I'm lost! Help!"

"We can't see you!" my sister yelled back.

My stomach squeezed. I couldn't see Ashley, either. I could *hear* her, but it was hard to know where her voice was coming from.

"Get me out of here!" I yelled.

I heard Kelly shout, "We'll get Jared!"

Jared? What could *he* do to save me and Wilbur?

I found out soon enough. Jared arrived, towering above the cornstalks! I stared up at him. *How is he doing that?* I wondered. Then I realized he was walking on stilts!

"Jared! Over here!" I yelled and waved my arms in the air.

Looking down, Jared spotted me right away. "I'm coming!" he called.

The cornstalks hid the stilts, so Jared looked as if he were walking in the air. As I watched him coming closer, he reminded me of something. But what? Then it hit me.

He reminded me of the ghost!

7

GHOST HAIR

"**F**ollow me!" Jared called.

I kept my eyes on him and pushed cornstalks aside. Wilbur followed me.

Jared was as good on the stilts as he was on a skateboard. He wasn't even wobbling. Finally Wilbur and I made it out of the cornfield.

"Welcome back!" Ashley cheered.

Wilbur squealed when he saw Ashley. She bent down and patted him on the head. Then she gave me a hug. As she did, I whispered in her ear, "I think I've found our ghost! It's Jared! Look how tall he is on those stilts."

Ashley pulled away and gave me a puzzled look. "But why would he—" Then she realized that Jared was standing nearby. "We'll talk later," she said to me.

I smiled up at Jared. "Thanks for rescuing me!"

"Lucky for you I have stilts, Mary-Kate," he said. He stayed on his stilts as we walked back across the road to the farmers' market. He was really good.

"Where did you get those stilts?" I asked Jared.

"My dad made them for me for a school talent show." Jared did a little fancy footwork, and Kelly clapped.

"What a show-off," Mitch muttered.

Ashley and I let the other three get ahead of us so we could discuss the case.

"I'm telling you. Jared is the 'ghost,'" I

insisted. "He can use his stilts to tower over the hedges of the maze."

Ashley pulled out her notebook and wrote *Jared*. She gazed at his name and shook her head. "I don't know, Mary-Kate," she said. "He doesn't have long blond hair."

"Maybe he wore a wig?" I offered.

"That's true," she said. "Okay. So he's a suspect."

Ashley and I joined Jared, Mitch, and Kelly near the corn stand. Ashley tucked her notebook under her arm and started brushing off my jacket. "Mary-Kate, what's this stuff all over you?"

"It's corn silk," Kelly told her. "You know, the long strands that cover the ears of corn inside the husks."

"Right." I remembered. "You use it for your doll hair."

Ashley gasped.

"Are you okay?" Kelly asked.

"Oh, sure," Ashley said quickly. She

grabbed my arm and pulled me away from the group. "Mary-Kate, don't these strands look familiar?"

I examined the corn silk. "It looks like the 'hair' we found in the maze!"

"Remember how I said the ghost hair didn't feel like real hair? It felt just like this!"

I nodded. "Kelly uses corn silk for doll hair. Maybe she used it for a wig too." I looked at Ashley. "She even has a motive."

Ashley nodded. "That's right," she said. "The reason she would want to scare everyone away from Mitch's maze is so they'll go to *her* maze instead. Kelly could definitely be the ghost."

Ashley opened her notebook again. "Now we have another suspect." She added a new name to our list: *Kelly*.

8

THE RETURN OF CHUCKLES

Ashley and I bought cups of hot apple cider from a nearby stand while Mitch went to buy himself a snack. We sat on a bale of hay and went over all the clues we had so far.

"I think we can officially cross off Mitch and the ghost from our list of suspects," Ashley said.

I nodded. "I agree."

"Okay, so who does that leave?"

"Greavy hates the maze, and he has a step stool that he could use to tower over the hedges," I said. "So he has motive *and* opportunity."

"True." She tapped her chin with her pencil. "We still have to see if his step stool matches the prints we found in the maze."

"Then there's Rachel," I said. "She wears a lot of pink, which might match the fluff we found, and she knows her way around the maze."

"And she has a motive—to scare her brother," Ashley said. "Mitch annoys her with all his practical jokes."

"Mitch annoys *everyone* with his practical jokes," I pointed out.

"We have a lot of suspects." Ashley said, looking down at her notebook. "Jared would be tall enough on his stilts to be the ghost," she said. "Kelly makes dolls with corn-silk hair, which is just like the 'hair' we found in the maze. She could have dressed up in white like a ghost and used the corn silk to make a wig for herself."

"She also has a motive," I reminded her. "If she can scare people away from Mitch's maze, she could get them to go to *her* maze instead."

"Only the ghost doesn't seem to scare anyone but Mitch," Ashley pointed out.

And me, I thought, but I didn't say that out loud.

I watched Jared horsing around on his stilts by the corn stand. Kelly laughed at his antics. "Maybe Kelly borrows Jared's stilts to play the ghost," I suggested.

"That's possible," Ashley said. "I wonder if Kelly knows how to walk on stilts."

"Let's find out." I stood up and waved. "Hey, Jared!" I called. "May I try your stilts?"

"Sure," Jared said. "I have to go get my little brother now anyway." He hopped off the stilts and handed them to me. Then he hurried away.

"Okay, here goes!" I got one foot up on one stilt with no problem. Then, holding on tightly, I hoisted myself up to get my other foot onto the little ledge on the other stilt. Suddenly I was a giant!

But only for about two seconds. Then both stilts started to wobble. I managed to hop off them before I tumbled to the ground.

Kelly clapped. "That was good for a first try."

I held the stilts out to Kelly. "Want a try?" I asked.

"Okay," Kelly said.

"Now we'll find out if she could be the ghost," I whispered to Ashley. We both watched eagerly as Kelly got up onto the stilts and started walking around.

"You're pretty good!" I told her.

"Thanks!" she replied. "Jared taught me how to use them!"

Ashley and I exchanged knowing looks.

Just then, Rachel strolled up to us, carrying two bags of fruit and vegetables. "What are you guys doing?" she asked.

"We're fooling around with Jared's stilts," Ashley said. "Do you want to try them?"

"No, thanks," Rachel said. "I have to baby-sit as soon as Jared shows up with Nicky."

"Jared just went to get him," I told her. "Are you sure you don't want to try the stilts? It's fun!"

"*No*," Rachel said.

I looked at Ashley. Was Rachel afraid of falling? Or was she avoiding the stilts because she didn't want us to know she could walk on them . . . just like the ghost?

Suddenly a terrible noise startled us. "*WAH-ha-ha-ha-ha-heeeeee!*"

"What was *that*?" Kelly asked.

I covered my ears with my hands, but I could still hear that awful, scratchy sound.

"*WAH-ha-ha-ha-ha-heeeeee!*"

My forehead creased. I had heard that horrible sound before.

Little Nicky ran up to Rachel, Jared trailing behind him. "Look, Rachel! Chuckles is back!" He held up a weird, ugly toy. It looked like an orange ball with popping eyes and a creepy smile. He squeezed it, and we heard the terrible noise again.

"*That's* his favorite toy?" Ashley asked me in a low voice.

"I bet he thinks tarantulas are cute too," I whispered back.

Nicky squeezed the toy again. This time I was sure: Chuckles and the ghost had the same laugh!

"Where did you find Chuckles?" I asked Nicky.

"Jared found him for me," the little boy said, looking happily up at his big brother.

"I wonder if that's what we saw Rachel giving Jared this morning," I said quietly to Ashley. "She could have borrowed it to make that horrible ghost laugh."

Ashley nodded. "And she certainly knows her way around the maze. We'll have to try again to find out if she has anything that matches the pink fluff we found."

"I'm sure she's the 'ghost,'" I said.

"We don't really have proof," Ashley reminded me. "She could have just found the toy, and we still don't know if she can walk on stilts."

"Let's try to find out some more." I turned to Rachel. "Nicky seems really happy to have his favorite toy back," I said to her.

Rachel glanced at Nicky. He was squeezing Chuckles over and over, giggling every time the toy laughed its awful laugh.

"I almost wish it had stayed lost," Rachel confessed. "That thing gives me the creeps."

"Is that why you had it in your desk drawer?" I asked. "To keep it away from Nicky for a while?" I watched her expression carefully.

She looked surprised. Then her eyes narrowed with suspicion. "How did you know that Chuckles was in my desk?" she asked. "Are you helping Mitch with some new prank?"

"No! Nothing like that," I assured her. "It's just that we saw you taking the toy from your desk drawer this morning when we were leaving your room . . . and then we saw you giving it to Jared when we passed his house on our way here."

Rachel shrugged. "I found the toy on the ground last night. I stopped at Nicky's house to return it on my way here."

It was a perfectly logical explanation. But I wasn't satisfied. So when Jared climbed back onto his stilts, I asked him if Rachel could try them.

"Sure," Jared said, and he hopped off.

Rachel glared at me. "I already told you I don't *want* to try Jared's stilts!"

"She's scared," Mitch said, returning from the snack stand with a caramel-covered apple and a bottle of ginger ale.

"I am not scared!" Rachel snapped.

"Are so," Mitch replied.

"Well, at least I'm not afraid of a silly story." Rachel raised her voice. "Hey, everybody!" she shouted. "My brother, Mitch, won't go in our maze! He's scared of the ghost!"

I could see that Mitch was embarrassed.

"I am *not*," Mitch said hotly.

"You are too!" Rachel laughed.

"I am not!" Mitch insisted.

"Then prove it," Rachel said. "Go into the maze . . . tonight."

"Okay, I will!" Mitch told her.

"What if you run into the ghost?" Rachel teased.

Mitch didn't answer.

Ashley leaned in to me. *"That's exactly what we'll be hoping for!"* she whispered.

9

BACK IN THE MAZE

As soon as the sun went down, Ashley and Mitch headed to the maze. I went to the barn. Other than Rachel's bedroom, the hayloft in the barn had the best view of the maze.

I climbed the ladder to the hayloft, dragging along a big camping flashlight and Mitch's binoculars. I crept to the window and peered through the binoculars. *Excellent!* From up here I could see right into the maze. I spotted Mitch and Ashley a few rows in. They had flashlights too.

Come on, ghost. Ready when you are.

I didn't have to wait long. Someone carrying a large shopping bag hurried to the maze entrance and stopped. It was too dark to tell who it was, even with the binoculars. I *could* see that he or she seemed impatient—glancing around, tapping one foot.

"What are you waiting for?" I whispered.

Then someone else raced up to the maze entrance. The two people talked, then scurried into the maze.

A few minutes later a white-draped figure with long blond hair rose up above the hedges, just one row away from Mitch and Ashley!

I raced out of the barn and dashed into the maze. Then I remembered: How was I going to find my way around?

"Ashley?" I yelled.

"Turn left, Mary-Kate!" Ashley called back to me.

So I went left and came around a corner.

I pointed my flashlight at the figure, just in time to see Ashley pull a white sheet off the "ghost."

"*Jared!*" Mitch cried.

A rustling sound behind Jared caught my attention. I aimed my flashlight toward the movement.

"And *Rachel*!" I shouted.

Rachel blinked from the flashlight's bright beam. She backed up against the hedge with a surprised look on her face. "Hey! Stop shining that thing in my eyes!" she complained.

I shined the light in a different direction. Rachel stepped forward, and her sweater got caught on the hedge. When she moved away from the bushes, a little piece of her sweater remained stuck on a branch.

"That's how you ruined your pink sweater too, right?" Ashley asked.

Rachel looked at the fluff. "Yeah," she replied. "That was my favorite sweater. I had to throw it away because it got ruined."

So that's why we didn't find it in her room, I thought.

"What's going on?" Mitch demanded. He looked at Rachel, then at Jared, then back at Rachel. "You guys are the ghost?"

They both nodded.

"That's why this mystery was so tricky to solve," I said. "We thought there was one ghost but really, there was a ghost *team*!"

Ashley nodded. "Rachel needed Jared on his stilts."

I pointed my flashlight at Jared. I had to bite my lip to keep from giggling. He looked so funny standing on his stilts wearing a corn-silk wig. "Nice wig," I said.

Jared shook his corn-silk hair. "I made it myself," he said proudly. "I got the idea from Kelly's corncob dolls with corn-silk hair."

Ashley reached down and picked up Nicky's toy from the ground. "And Rachel used Chuckles to make that awful laugh."

"I couldn't squeeze Chuckles because I

needed both hands to work the stilts," Jared explained.

"And the *stilts* were what made those weird tracks in the ground," I pointed out. "Not Greavy's step stool."

Mitch shook his head. "Why did you do this?" he asked the pair.

"We were sick of all your pranks!" Rachel told him. "So when I heard about the ghost legend, I figured this was a way to pull a prank on *you*."

Jared nodded. "After all the pranks you've pulled on us, you deserved to get fooled. This was payback!"

Mitch sighed. "Okay, I get it. Let's say we're even."

"And let's say no more pranks from now on!" Rachel said.

"Agreed," Mitch said.

Using my flashlight to guide us, we all made our way to the exit from the maze.

Another mystery solved!

I still had one question to ask. "How did you guys make those glowing eyes in the hedges?"

"What glowing eyes?" Rachel asked.

Ashley and I exchanged a look.

"Those!" Mitch cried, pointing up to the hedges above our heads.

"They're so real," I said. "What did you make them out of?"

"Uh . . . I didn't make anything with glowing eyes," Rachel told us. She turned to Jared. "Did you?"

"No, not me," Jared replied.

Ashley shot me a worried look. Rachel and Jared sounded as if they were telling the truth.

"M-maybe there really *is* a ghost, after all!" Mitch said nervously.

Suddenly, the hedges rustled. My hand shook as I pointed the flashlight toward the noise.

And then we saw it: a big barn owl hiding in the hedges! The large bird stared down at us, blinked a few times, then flew away.

It was quiet for a moment, then we all burst out laughing.

"You know, Rachel, our prank was really great," Jared said as we headed out of the maze. "But we made one mistake."

"What was that?" Rachel asked.

"The blond-haired girl's ghost is supposed to appear every *ten* years," Jared said.

"Yeah, so?" Rachel replied.

"So the high school opened *nine* years ago," Jared said.

Mitch gulped. "You mean next fall there could be a *real* ghost in the maze? One who's searching for a red-haired boy?"

Ashley and I looked at each other. "I guess I know where the Trenchcoat Twins will be *next* Halloween!" Ashley said.

I nodded. "Solving another ghostly mystery!" I said with a big grin.

Hi from both of us,

Ashley and I were so excited to visit Washington, D.C., during Christmas vacation. We were going to join a Hidden Holiday Riddle Hunt! Since we're both so good at solving riddles and tracking down clues, we thought winning would be easy!

But then we discovered somebody was cheating! Our riddle was stolen and replaced with a fake one. The fake riddle sent us on a wild-goose chase—well, a wild-*dog* chase was more like it! Ashley and I had to stop searching for hidden riddles—and start searching for a riddle thief instead! Want to find out what happened? Check out the next page for a sneak peek at *The New Adventures of Mary-Kate and Ashley: The Case Of The Hidden Holiday Riddle.*

See you next time!

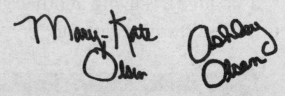

A sneak peek at our next mystery…

The Case Of The
HIDDEN HOLIDAY RIDDLE

"Come on!" I called to Ashley. "We need to check the doghouse for our next riddle!"

I raced downstairs into Sarah Jordan's huge foyer. Ashley and I were staying at Sarah's house with Great-grandma Olive during Christmas vacation. Sarah's father is an old friend of Great-grandma Olive. We were in the middle of a Hidden Holiday Riddle Hunt.

Ashley followed me

downstairs. "The doghouse?" she asked. "You want to go to . . . *Tea and Crumpet's doghouse*?"

The Jordans owned two big German Shepherd guard dogs named Tea and Crumpet. They were kept in a large doghouse in the backyard.

"Don't worry," I assured her. "Great-grandma Olive would never give us a clue that sent us to the doghouse if the dogs were dangerous."

"I guess not," Ashley said slowly. "But Tea and Crumpet *look* dangerous. And they have such sharp teeth!"

"We'll be *okay*," I said, pulling her by the sleeve. "Stop worrying. We'll just slip in, grab our next riddle, and slip out."

We headed toward the doghouse. I could see Tea and Crumpet lying quietly next to their doghouse with their heads down. Their stomachs slowly moved up and down. Up and down. "They're asleep!" I said, lowering my voice. "Come on!"

"Good doggy," Ashley whispered as she tiptoed behind me. "Nice doggy! Stay sleeping, doggy. Good doggy!"

"Awww. See how sweet they look?" I tried to joke as we stepped around the sleeping dogs and crept up to the doggy door.

"Just hurry up!" Ashley whispered. "See if our next riddle is inside!"

I bent down to stick my head through the doggy door and I bumped my head into the doghouse!

"*Yeeeowch!*" I cried, rubbing my sore head.

Ashley's eyes widened in horror. "Shhhh!" she whispered.

But it was too late. Tea and Crumpet both woke up from all the noise. They raised their heads and stared straight at us.

Crumpet began to growl.

Tea began to snarl.

At the moment, they did not look sweet *at all*. In fact, they looked *angry*.

Without missing a beat, Ashley took off toward the house. "Mary-Kate!" she yelled. "Come on!"

"I'm right behind you!" I yelled back, running faster than ever before. I knew the dogs were chasing us because I could hear them *panting*. I ran for my life!

Suddenly, Tea and Crumpet stopped. Both dogs had reached the end of their chains! They couldn't go any farther. Ashley and I were safe. We collapsed on the ground and tried to catch our breath.

"What's . . . going . . . on?" Ashley asked, in between gasps of air. "How could Great-grandma Olive send us *there*?"

I couldn't believe it either. I still had Great-grandma Olive's riddle clutched in my hand. I smoothed it out and took a closer look. That's when I saw it.

"Ashley, look!" I cried. "This riddle wasn't written by Great-grandma Olive!" I showed her. "This riddle is a *fake*!"

ary-Kate and Ashley

Win an "Apple iPod®"
Sweepstakes

A PORTABLE DIGITAL MUSIC PLAYER!

Record hours of music from your favorite CDs or online music sites! Load it up and carry it in your pocket!

Mail to: **THE NEW ADVENTURES OF MARY-KATE AND ASHLEY**
Apple iPod® SWEEPSTAKES
c/o HarperEntertainment
Attention: Children's Marketing Department
10 East 53rd Street, New York, NY 10022

No purchase necessary.

Name: _____

Address: _____

City: _____ State: _____ Zip: _____

Phone: _____ Age: _____

HarperEntertainment
An Imprint of HarperCollins*Publishers*
www.harpercollins.com

DUALSTAR PUBLICATIONS

PARACHUTE PRESS

The New Adventures of Mary-Kate and Ashley
Apple iPod® Sweepstakes
OFFICIAL RULES:

1. NO PURCHASE OR PAYMENT NECESSARY TO ENTER OR WIN.

2. How to Enter. To enter, complete the official entry form or hand print your name, address, age and phone number along with the words "New Adventures Apple iPod® Sweepstakes" on a 3" x 5" card and mail to: New Adventures Apple iPod® Sweepstakes, c/o HarperEntertainment, Attn: Children's Marketing Department, 10 East 53rd Street, New York, NY 10022. Entries must be received no later than February 28, 2005. Enter as often as you wish, but each entry must be mailed separately. One entry per envelope. Partially completed, illegible, or mechanically reproduced entries will not be accepted. Sponsor are not responsible for lost, late, mutilated, illegible, stolen, postage due, incomplete or misdirected entries. All entries become the property of Dualstar Entertainment Group, LLC, and will not be returned.

3. Eligibility. Sweepstakes open to all legal residents of the United States (excluding Colorado and Rhode Island) who are between the ages of five and fifteen on February 28, 2005 excluding employees and immediate family members of HarperCollins Publishers, Inc., ("HarperCollins"), Parachute Properties and Parachute Press, Inc., and their respective subsidiaries and affiliates, officers, directors, shareholders, employees, agents, attorneys, and other representatives and their immediate families (individually and collectively, "Parachute"), Dualstar Entertainment Group, LLC, and its subsidiaries and affiliates, officers, directors, shareholders, employees, agents, attorneys, and other representatives and their immediate families (individually and collectively, "Dualstar"), and their respective parent companies, affiliates, subsidiaries, advertising, promotion and fulfillment agencies, and the persons with whom each of the above are domiciled. All applicable federal, state and local laws and regulations apply. Offer void where prohibited or restricted by law.

4. Odds of Winning. Odds of winning depend on the total number of entries received. Approximately 300,000 sweepstakes announcements published. All prizes will be awarded. Winner will be randomly drawn on or about March 15, 2005, by HarperCollins, whose decision is final. Potential winner will be notified by mail and will be required to sign and return an affidavit of eligibility and release of liability within 14 days of notification. Prizes won by minors will be awarded to parent or legal guardian who must sign and return all required legal documents. By acceptance of their prize, winners consent to the use of their names, photographs, likeness, and biographical information by HarperCollins, Parachute, Dualstar, and for publicity purposes without further compensation except where prohibited.

5. Grand Prize. One Grand Prize Winner will win an Apple iPod.® Approximate retail value of prize totals $500.00.

6. Prize Limitations. All prizes will be awarded. Only one prize will be awarded per individual, family, or household. Prizes are non-transferable and cannot be sold or redeemed for cash. No cash substitute is available. Any federal, state, or local taxes are the responsibility of the winner. Sponsor may substitute prize of equal or greater value, if necessary, due to availability.

7. Additional terms: By participating, entrants agree a) to the official rules and decisions of the judges, which will be final in all respects; and to waive any claim to ambiguity of the official rules and b) to release, discharge, and hold harmless HarperCollins, Parachute, Dualstar, and their respective parent companies, affiliates, subsidiaries, employees and representatives and advertising, promotion and fulfillment agencies from and against any and all liability or damages associated with acceptance, use, or misuse of any prize received or participation in any Sweepstakes-related activity or participation in this Sweepstakes.

8. Dispute Resolution. Any dispute arising from this Sweepstakes will be determined according to the laws of the State of New York, without reference to its conflict of law principles, and the entrants consent to the personal jurisdiction of the State and Federal courts located in New York County and agree that such courts have exclusive jurisdiction over all such disputes.

9. Winner Information. To obtain the name of the winner, please send your request and a self-addressed stamped envelope (residents of Vermont may omit return postage) to New Adventures Apple iPod® Sweepstakes Winner, c/o HarperEntertainment, 10 East 53rd Street, New York, NY 10022 after April 15, 2005, but no later than October 15, 2005.

10. Sweepstakes Sponsor: HarperCollins Publishers, Inc. Apple© Corporation is not affiliated, connected or associated with this Sweepstakes in any manner and bears no responsibility for the administration of this Sweepstakes.

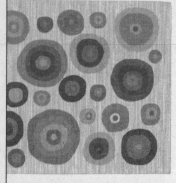

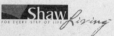

Travel the world with **Mary-Kate** and **Ashley**
www.mary-kateandashley.com

Mary-Kate Olsen   Ashley Olsen

new york minute
the movie

Experience the same hilarious trials and tribulations as Roxy and Jane did in their feature film *New York Minute*.

Bonus Movie Mini-Poster!

⟶The New Adventures of⟵ MARY-KATE & ASHLEY ™

DETECTIVE TRICK

THE FLASHLIGHT CODE

You can send secret signals to your friends using a flashlight. Just make sure you have plenty of batteries! Here are some important blink signals:

1. *Help!*–Move the flashlight beam from right to left quickly.

2. *Come here!*–Make a circle with the light beam.

3. *Are you okay?*–Blink the flashlight three times in a row.

4. *Yes!*–Make one blink.

5. *No!*–Make two blinks.

Now see if you can come up with some secret flash signals of your own!

www.mary-kateandashley.com

From
The Case Of The HAUNTED MAZE

⟶The New Adventures of⟵ MARY-KATE & ASHLEY ™

DETECTIVE TRICK

HIDE IT IN PLAIN SIGHT

Want to hide something from a snoopy friend, brother, or sister? It's easy—just hide your stuff in plain sight. Here are a few ideas:

1. Remove one of your videos/DVDs from its container. Put your secret stuff inside. Then slip the box back in its place with the others. No one will think to look there.

2. Don't throw away your empty checkers box. Put all your secret stuff inside. Stack the box at the bottom of a pile of other board games. It will be "hidden" in plain sight!

3. An ordinary book is the perfect place to hide secret letters. Just slip the letters in between the pages and put the book back on your bookshelf. Even the sneakiest snoop won't look there!

Look for our next mystery . . .
The Case Of The HIDDEN HOLIDAY RIDDLE